Illustrated by
Frances Ives
To Liz and Simon, for always being there.

Editorial consultancy by Justine Smith
Edited by Jocelyn Norbury
Designed by Jack Clucas
Cover design by Angie Allison

With special thanks to Philippa Wingate

Published in Great Britain in 2018 by Michael O'Mara Books Limited,
9 Lion Yard, Tremadoc Road, London SW4 7NQ

W www.mombooks.com/lom   f Michael O'Mara Books   🐦 @OMaraBooks

Copyright @ Michael O'Mara Books Limited 2018

A CIP catalogue record for this book is available from the British Library.

HB ISBN: 978-1-910552-82-7
PB ISBN: 978-1-910552-84-1

1 3 5 7 9 10 8 6 4 2

This book was printed in July 2018 by
Leo Paper Products Ltd, Heshan Astros Printing Limited, Xuantan Temple Industrial Zone,
Gulao Town, Heshan City, Guangdong Province, China.

Once, there was a boy called Eric,
who lived in a forest.

Eric loved to help his mother in their garden and play with his animal friends.

He felt like the happiest boy in the world.

At night, he liked to look up at the sky.

"I see the moon, so high above, shining on me and the friends I love," thought Eric.

One day, when winter had turned the forest white with frost ...

"... Eric's mother took him on a long journey ..."

... to the city.

Eric and his mother walked through busy streets to their new house.

That night, when he gazed up at the moon,
it looked so different that it made Eric sad.

He missed his life in the
forest more than ever.

"Maybe the moon, so high above, is shining on me and the friends I love."

The next morning, Eric told the cat who lived in his house all about his forest friends and what they liked to do together.

Eric decided to go out and explore the city.

He got to know the corners,

and the creatures,

the children,

and the challenges.

He explored the city from top to bottom.

Eric showed his new
friends how to plant a
garden and help it grow.

He even got used to the moon.

One spring day, the time came for Eric and his mother to leave the great city and go back home.

Eric told his forest friends about his adventures and the new animals and children he had met.

That night Eric looked
up at the sky and thought ...

"I know that the moon, so high above,
is shining on me and the friends I love.
Whether we live in the forest or play in the park,
we are all joined together by the light in the dark."